To Victoria, with love
~ T. K.

For my Mom
~ L. H.

tiger tales
5 River Road, Suite 128, Wilton, CT 06897
Published in the United States 2016
Originally published in Great Britain 2016
by Little Tiger Press
Text copyright © 2016 Timothy Knapman
Illustrations copyright © 2016 Laura Hughes
ISBN-13: 978-1-68010-030-3
ISBN-10: 1-68010-030-0
Printed in China
LTP/1400/1431/0216

For more insight and activities, visit us at www.tigertalesbooks.com

GOOD NIGHT
TIGER

by Timothy Knapman • Illustrated by Laura Hughes

tiger tales

It was the middle of the night,
but **Emma** couldn't sleep . . .

because of all the
BELLOWING
and STOMPING

and TRUMPETING
and GROWLING!

"The **animals** must have escaped
from the **ZOO!**" she cried.

But there was no one on the street
except the next door neighbor's cat.

Emma looked **under** the bed,

on **top** of
the wardrobe,

and through **all** her
toys and clothes,

until at last she saw
that the **noise** was
coming from . . .

. . . the **animals** in her wallpaper!

The gorilla BELLOWED

and the hippo STOMPED

and the elephant TRUMPETED

and the tiger GROWLED

until Emma shouted, "Go to

sleep!"

"We've tried and tried, but we **can't!**" said the tiger.

"Well, maybe I can help you," said Emma.

And she grabbed a chair

and **climbed** up

into the wallpaper.

"Have you taken your **bath** yet?"
asked Emma.

"No," said the tiger.

"Well, **no wonder** you can't sleep!" said Emma.

But there wasn't a bathtub **anywhere** in the jungle. "We could always use the watering hole," said the tiger.

So the hippo scrubbed behind his ears.

The elephant used his trunk to give himself a shower.

And the gorilla shampooed his fur until it was soft and shiny . . . .

But when the tiger jumped in,
he landed on the crocodiles!
What a RUCKUS!

SNAP!

"A bath like **that** won't help you get to sleep," said Emma.
"How about some **hot chocolate?**"

"Yes, please!"
said the tiger.

But there was no hot chocolate **anywhere** in the jungle.

"We could always use mud," said the tiger.

So the gorilla mixed it
very carefully.

And the elephant used his trunk
to pour it into little cups.

It smelled **horrible.**

But when Emma and the tiger took
a drink, it **actually** tasted . . .

"A drink like **that** won't help you
get to sleep," said Emma. "But what else can I do?"

Emma tried **everything**.
She gave them a bear to cuddle . . .

but the bear didn't want to be bothered, so he ran away.

She started to sing them a lullaby, but all the animals in the jungle joined in, and it became too

LOUD!

She even tried to turn the lights off,
but she couldn't find a switch **anywhere**.

"And we're
STILL not tired!"

said the animals.

"I don't know what to do!" cried Emma at last.
"You can't sleep, and that means
I can't sleep, and I'm
EXHAUSTED!"

"Is there anything else we can try?"
asked the tiger.

And then Emma had a **wonderful** idea.

"We can read a **bedtime story!**" she said.

"Yes, please!" cried the animals.
"We've never heard a bedtime story!"

So Emma told them a story about some animals
who escaped from the zoo, the little girl who found them,
and the **great big adventure** they had before
they all went to bed.

When she was finished,
the gorilla, the hippo,
and the elephant
were **fast asleep.**

Emma yawned.
"I'm still wide awake," she said.

"How about a **good-night cuddle?**" said the tiger.

"Yes, please!"
said Emma.

"Good night, Emma."
"Good night, Tiger."

The next morning when Emma woke up,
the animals were smiling at her
from the wallpaper.
Everyone except the **tiger**.

Emma found him curled up on her bed.
And he was **still** fast asleep.

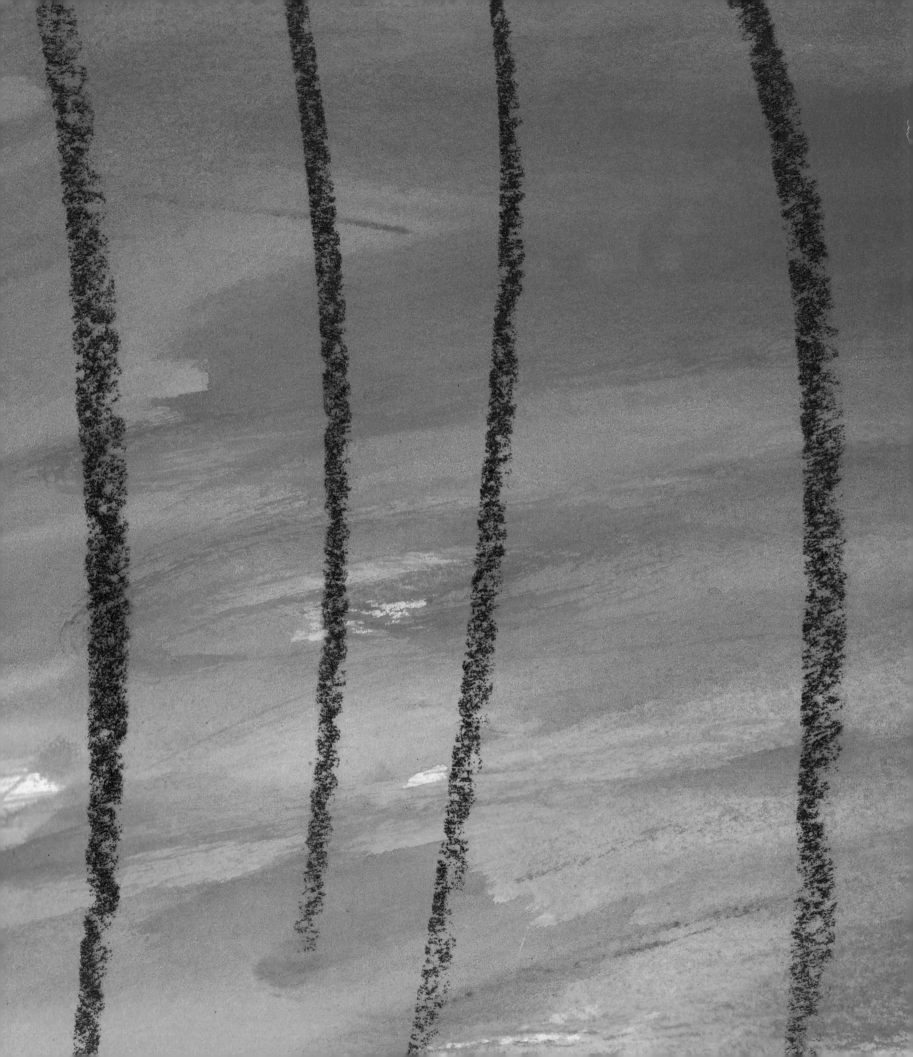